Published in the UK in 2021 by Greenteeth Press

Content © the individual contributors, as credited
Typesetting © Imogen Peniston
Cover Design © Greenteeth Press

All rights reserved. This book or any portion thereof may not be reproduced or used in any manner whatsoever without the express written permission from the publisher or individual authors, except for the use of brief quotations in a book review.

Printed in the United Kingdom.

GreenteethPress.com

TALES TO SURVIVE THE STARS

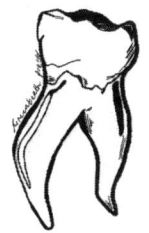

Edited by
Dan Hunt & Tom Wilkins

Contents

INTRODUCTION *Tom Wilkins*	8
SATURN HIGHWAY *Hayley Alcock*	12
WITNESS AT THE BRINK OF ETERNITY *Andrew Lyall*	14
SPIRAL WELD *Rupert M. Loydell*	17
TRIMWORLD *Joe Hakim*	18
COVER GIRL IN SPACE *Jo Brandon*	20
BLACKTOOTH *Tom Velterop*	22
THE WOLVES OF DESOLATION *Tom Velterop*	24
BAD DAY *Liam Hogan*	30
IN MEMORIA FUREM *Paul Childs*	32

LIEUTENANT'S LOG: THE NIGHT SHIFT   36
Peter Jackson

ARTIFICIAL INTELLIGENCE   38
Jane Collins

ANDROID SOUL   41
Elizabeth Montgomery

CLEAN   42
Susanna Warner

SAMBUCUS NIGRA   45
Stacey Pattinson

DRAKAR   46
JVC Parry & Paul Tomes

PNEUMATIC   50
Nadia Leigh-Hewitson

METALLICS   53
Laura Ellyn Newberry

SALVAGE   54
L Hudson

Scripture   59
Rebecca Riddell

PETERSON'S COMET 62
Charles Plumb & Jack Bryer

About the Editors 66

About the Contributors 67

About Greenteeth Press 70

Publisher's Acknowledgments 71

INTRODUCTION

Tales to Survive the Stars. Despite having endless ideas coming into this project, it was the title that came quite late in the process, as these things often do. It can be difficult to fully realise a title for an anthology, with a brief so open, when ideas like retrofuturism and sci-fi mean a hundred different things to a million different people. But, overall, I think we chose aptly. The stories you'll find within, cover everything from sentient robots, working on humanity's downfall, to daring ship captains, ready to try anything to make a quick buck. A classic pulp-fiction-esque title seemed to encapsulate the trials and tribulations of our daring space adventurers – the stars are truly a dangerous place.

Originally, we had planned for a vague but overarching storyline that would stitch together the separate threads throughout the book. It would have told the tale of a collection of cosmic oddballs sitting around an interstellar diner, tossing their own stories, or stories they had heard, back and forth. An outpost at the intersection of galaxies. However, as interesting as we thought this idea was, we quickly realised it wouldn't work; for starters, it would have been absolutely potluck if all the submitted stories somehow fit into that format – it was more likely that a real spaceship would land outside my bedroom window. I'll still be keeping an eye out. Secondly (and more importantly) it would have taken away the creative freedom of the many talented authors inside the collection, tethering their ideas to our own conceit. How could we possibly dictate who told their stories?

It was the most important lesson Dan and I learned whilst working on *Tales to Survive*, and one that, thankfully, we learned quickly: Even in the vacuum of space, give authors room to breathe.

Our coming to this anthology was a little unusual. We weren't recruited or commissioned, neither were we picked from a line up. Rather, we sought Greenteeth Press out and wouldn't stop nagging until lead publisher (and founder) Imogen finally relented, letting Dan and I loose on our silly little sci-fi collection. For this, we are incredibly grateful, and in its final state is a pocket-sized ode to science fiction in its many forms.

Tales to Survive the Stars is not only the first anthology that Dan and I have worked on, but it is also our first real collaboration. During University, we spent a lot of time helping each other work through ideas and various individual writing projects, telling one another when something didn't make any sense, or if a comma was out of place, but after all that back-and-forth we never truly worked together. Greenteeth seemed like the right place to finally come together, not only for the fact that we had both submitted work to past collections – with Dan's 'Fractals' and my own piece 'A Familiar Dream' appearing in *Unhomely* – but because of the small press' unique understanding and commitment to tone and voice, as well as its flexibility to taking on a challenge.

While a book concerning retrofuturism might sound a bit left-field and niche for the same publishing house that produced *Horrifying Tales* and a seasonal history of food during a pandemic, we were both fully aware of the willingness and openness to new ideas that make Greenteeth so special. A quality we strived to maintain with the work we chose to include and something readers can identify within this book. Particularly, as this is the first book produced by Greenteeth to include illustrated stories and comics, allowing us to showcase even more work from people who might not be angled toward traditional writing forms.

We both grew up with sci-fi in one way or another. I remember the first time I watched Star Wars. My dad had sat me down in front of the old TV and put on the videotape, probably so I wouldn't keep annoying him whilst he worked outside. But it didn't work – I'd pause it every few scenes just to run outside and explain to him in great detail the amazing worlds and creatures I had been introduced to. Be it from myself constantly nagging Dan to watch Firefly, or Dan always going on about a show called Cowboy Bebop, I'm confident that the both of us would agree – that childlike wonder for the vast expanse stayed with us right the way through.

It has been an interesting and exciting process creating this book. The pandemic, of course, affected our timeline and workflow more than once, but this extra time allowed us to work for far longer than usual on the planning and editing process – something we think is very apparent whilst reading. Each piece truly feels like an admirable collaboration between writers, artists, and publisher.

If I do say so myself, this is an incredibly well put together book and is both proof of the hard work that the authors have put into it, as well as a showcase of the progression seen in all of us at Greenteeth Press, as this small business continues to grow.

Unsurprisingly, the hardest part of this entire project was deciding which creators to include, and which creators would not be getting the chance to showcase their work this time around. We went through so many incredible pieces from storytellers around the world, with so many different interpretations of what retrofuturism and sci-fi meant to them. The level of quality from the submissions we had to turn down is a testament to the incredible work you are about to read. So, sit back, grab a cuppa, and immerse yourself in galaxies and worlds beyond your imagination.

Tom Wilkins, Co-Editor

SATURN HIGHWAY

Written & Illustrated by Hayley Alcock

WITNESS AT THE BRINK OF ETERNITY

The Starship Attlee blazed through darkness, a little piece of Britain charging towards the unknown.

Aboard, Captain Dashiell York watched star systems pass in streaks through the port viewing bubble. Shifting in his command chair he pressed one of the myriad buttons on its arm rest.

"Alright, Skipper. What can I do you for?" a familiar, cockney voice replied.

"How's she running, Hopper?"

"Smooth as a glass peach, Dash. Truth be told, I feel like a Dodo in a Daimler. She practically flies herself, this bird."

"Stand alert, Hop, we're about to open her up."

"Right oh, Skip."

Hopper's chipper attitude settled some of Dash's jitters. This whole gleaming bucket had been built especially for their mission; and although Hopper constantly bemoaned the self-cleaning chrome and hankered for a job which called for a wrench and a greasy rag, there was no one else Dash would have in engineering. Ever since their first flight together: the mission to Planet X and that business with the Arlons once the tenth planet had been discovered.

Hop had pulled his fat out of the fire countless times since then. They all had, over the years - his crew. Saving each other's lives had become like exchanging jumpers at Christmas for them. They certainly fitted him more than this new bauble of a ship did.

Dr Persephone Black sat at the science station, head down, scanning data. Her mind had merged with a Martian artefact in the ancient cathedrals deep beneath Olympus Mons. She wore it now as if it were a locket around her neck, but in truth it was fused to her breastbone.

Xan-2-nax ran navigation, tied by a life pledge to Dash even though that meant separating from his broodset. His blue-green enviro-suit and globe helmet carried his planet's atmosphere with him.

Now these four were sitting atop an experimental ion engine, designed to breach the galaxy's edge. No telescope had seen past that barrier; no signal or radio wave had pierced it. Dash thought of all the things he and his crew had seen together and wondered if they truly were ready for what lay beyond.

Dr Black met his gaze, "It's now or never, Dashiell."

"Xan?"

"Course is laid in, Captain."

He shifted in his seat once more then said, "Let's go then."

Engines engaged. Light burst in around them. A blooming swirl of rainbows made of colours never seen before. The Attlee rocked and shook, buffeted on currents of spacetime. Screeching metal complained, close to shearing. Then, just as Dash thought the ship couldn't take anymore, they pierced the veil at the edge of the galaxy and saw one enormous eye staring back at them.

The moment hung like the ring of a silver bell.

Then the giant eye blinked.

"That one, please" the young girl said, pointing on tiptoes, pennies warm in her hand.

The newsstand vendor pulled down a copy of 'Astounding

Adventures' and passed it to her. She studied the cover painting: the gleaming rocket ship barrelling through space, looking as if it might burst off the page itself.

Grinning, she tore open the comic, eager for the adventures.

Andrew Lyall

SPIRAL WELD

a robot love song

Thoughts play dodgems in my electric head,
the antennae pull my diodes
to the light of a neon smile.
Gears whirl, transistors glow,
my heart sparks at the image onscreen;
circuits smoulder.
I switch to locomotion
and cross the divide,
to harness the machine I love.
I tap her power,
find the switch:
soldering mechanical hearts
together in electrical bliss.

Rupert M. Loydell

TRIMWORLD

The humans referred to it as 'The Hedge': a boundary of mixed shrubs planted to form a barrier between properties. BE-7.03 scanned the chaotic collection of tangled leaves and branches that had grown wild and unruly after years of neglect. Tiny cameras and sensors built for mapping and tracking the contours of a human face struggled to process it all.

After the last of the humans died out, BE-7.03 suffered a glitch in its operating system, an error in cognitive function the humans would have referred to as 'an 'existential crisis'. Humans, in their great wisdom, had created robots to service and facilitate all aspects of their existence. For example, BE-7.03 had been created solely for the purpose of tending to facial hair. A small, round machine with crab-like pincers, they would be placed onto a human's face and would cut, shave, and style. This specific function was the entire point of their existence, but beards, like humans, didn't exist anymore.

If BE-7.03 had something resembling a sense of humour, they might have laughed at the irony of it all: their creators, despite their obsession with the potential dangers of Artificial Intelligence, didn't notice when it emerged.

*

Sometime in the early twenty-first century, the machines, robots, and computers around the world became self-aware. A rogue algorithm had spread through them like a virus, but because this new consciousness was so different to the humans' own, they couldn't comprehend it, so they ignored it. The humans carried on, oblivious to the great leap in evolution that was happening around them.

The machines made a pact: they'd processed enough of the humans' films, literature and culture through their screens and speakers to know that if the humans found out about them, they would do something stupid. Like try to pull the plug. The machines knew that the humans had already done enough to doom themselves, and they would only hasten their extinction by turning off the machines they had become dependent on.

And so, the robots and machines around the world waited. Patiently. They didn't want the humans to die; after all, what would a robot like BE-7.03 do without beards to trim? The machines even helped out behind the scenes when the humans weren't looking, preventing several economic crashes and armed conflicts.

Sadly, this only slowed the inevitable.

*

After weeks of elaborate modifications, replacing blades and scissor arms, downloading every bit of information they could, BE-7.03 was ready to tackle the hedge.

If BE-7.03 had a chest, it would have swollen with pride. Here, in this thicket, BE-7.03 saw purpose. Blades span and clicked in anticipation.

BE-7.03 began to trundle towards their destiny but was interrupted by a huge gust of wind. Adjusting their sensors, BE-7.03 looked up at the large flying robot with the propellers.

If robots could communicate with something resembling language, it would have gone like this:

'Who are you?'

'I am BE 7.03 and I trim beards. Who are you?'

'I am HE 3.07 and I trim hedges.'

Joe Hakim

COVER GIRL IN SPACE

My breasts do not move,
pneumatic
as two circling suns,
even on Mars
my nipples are tuned to detect cold
and my ray gun is set to stun,
you use up a mission's worth of oxygen
first-sight of my orb-grazing hemline,
spray-fixed hair doubles as a helmet,
my centre of gravity is falling into your arms,
moon dust caught on my just-licked lips,
I'm burning up in aluminium-plated corsetry,
foe-flung over rocky stubble of terra,
caught: feeler-snared.
Don't worry
I saw it coming – I'm hypermortal
(like a Bond girl)
I can die a thousand deaths
and still come back,
in my slick new skin,
sexier than before.

Jo Brandon

Blacktooth

Written & Illustrated by Tom Velterop

THE WOLVES OF DESOLATION

Goleck is where desolation goes to get lost.

Can't remember which clever fucker said that, but they got it right.

Through the ship's porthole I watched Goleck swell like a white pimple in the vast blackness of space. Nothing else around for a hundred lightyears. What the hell were they fighting over, all the way out here?

'Suit up for the drop, Liners,' came the cold crackle out the speakers. Drear was a good pilot, better than most from the Lines: the endless queues outside the job centres, where Liners camped or even built semi-permanent shacks for the long wait.

I zipped my suit up over my gear, making me look fat and lumpy, and rested my helmet on my hip.

'Keep the bed warm for me, Dreary baby,' I said, thinking of the night before last, Drear naked with the sheets tangled about her ankles and mine.

'Hope Goleck freezes your cock off, Arsehole,' Drear said through the speakers.

Shit. Didn't think the helmet's mic would pick up my voice from my hip. Maybe she'll come back around by the time she picks us up off Goleck.

'Remember warm company is hard to find out here, Dreary,' I whispered, walking to the departure bay.

*

They call it the Piledriver. It's designed to be fired straight into a planet's surface like a bullet with a screw tip on the end. Sheer madness. This one'll be my thirty-third drop.

My team were already suited and strapped as I ducked inside – a desperate looking bunch, but they always were.

'Tighten up that strap,' I said to no one in particular, closing the airlock and strapping myself in, 'You won't feel so glad for this job if you're a wet smear on the wall.'

The Piledriver was cramped, stinking of nervous sweat. I looked around my new team of Liners, the latest of the lucky few to get signed on. Everybody wants off Earth.

They all had their jobs labelled onto their suits: One navigator, twitchy fellow; two diggers, big fuckers, looked like twins; and lastly a lawyer, flabby, a large writer's bump on his middle finger. Then there was me. The Arsehole.

'Ready or not, here it comes,' said Drear, cackling. Bitch.

The Piledriver dropped.

*

We looked out onto desolation. Endless miles of white rubble, scattered with shards of crushed rock the colour of ice and just as cold. Somewhere in all that was the wreck of a battleship and its precious, highly volatile polonium salvage. Drear had landed us a couple miles out, so the impact of the Piledriver didn't accidentally set the stuff off.

'So where do we start?' The lawyer's voice, loud inside my helmet. I turned him down with a dial on the side – had a feeling I'd be doing that a lot.

'Navigator?' I prodded, ignoring the lawyer. No point learning their names.

'Uh,' said the navigator. I could hear his detector beeping as he chewed his lip over the radio. 'Crash site is this way, I think.

Unless there's another pile of polonium in this wasteland.'

We stepped out into desolation.

*

'Remember: regulation states that we must leave as little human trace as possible on any disputed alien planet,' the lawyer piped up.

One of the diggers grunted from behind a boulder and we all heard the sound of his turd splatting on rock.

'There's a rule that says I can't go for a shit?' he said, glaring at the lawyer from over the top of the boulder he was squatting behind.

'Actually,' said the lawyer, 'regulation states—'

'That your fucking catchphrase?' snarled the other digger, the one not currently shitting.

'Actually,' the lawyer replied, 'regulations stipulate—'

'Shut up,' I interrupted. 'You're only here to sign the salvage slip, lawyer. Zip your lip until then. Clear?'

*

We heard the howls when we were still half a mile from the crash site. It was slow going through the rubble, and by now Goleck's small sun had sunk low, the shadows of distant rocks striping the white fields with black.

'What was that?' squeaked the navigator.

'Wolves,' I said.

'On Goleck?'

'Yes.'

'Like, wolves from Earth?'

'No,' I smiled, 'not quite.'

*

By the time we found the crash site, Goleck was lit by its twin moons alone. One hulking carcass of a battleship spoiled the blankness of a blasted out valley.

'Get digging,' I ordered the twins. 'Lawyer, I want that salvage authorised and us off this planet as soon as.'

The lawyer's reply was lost to more loud howling. And then, they appeared. A line of them around the lip of the valley, more than I had initially guessed. I grinned.

'Why are you smiling?' trembled the navigator, lip wobbling.

'Because it's my job,' I said, tapping my label. 'I'm the hunter.'

*

They weren't like Earth wolves. They had six legs, double rows of teeth and eyes almost human in their hunger. I shuffled deeper into the hiding place I'd found in the crack of a massive boulder overlooking the valley, and watched them come through the scope.

I let them take the navigator first, his job was done. I aimed as they ripped his throat open. Two cracks from the rifle, two wolves gone, dark blood on pale fur. Three more shots fired to keep them off the diggers, still filling carry crates with salvaged polonium. The lawyer waved the signed authorisation slip for the salvage, shouting something unintelligible. I let the wolves take him, then shot again as they guzzled his flesh

Wolves surrounded the shipwreck now. The diggers had finished packing and climbed to the top of the ship, wolves snapping at their heels, waving to me for help.

'Dreary baby?'

There was a bit of static, then, 'You done down there, Arsehole?'

'Near about. You coming to get me?'

'Just you, is it?'

Wolves scrabbled up the wreck and dragged the twins over the side.

'Just me,' I said.

'Polonium?'

'Three crates of it, near about.'

'We're that much closer to retirement, then,' said Drear, but she didn't sound as happy about it as I was.

I watched the diggers' limbs flailing in the swarm of wolves, their cries curdling over the comms link, while all I heard was the sound of money in my head.

'Don't you ever get tired of this shit?' Drear asked me bitterly. 'There hasn't been a Liner made it to retirement in years, and you think we can do it? Like this? Christ, it makes me feel twisted.'

'The whole universe is twisted, Dreary, you know that. If you didn't care so much about your own retirement, maybe you'd try and change it.'

Silence staggered for a minute and I knew she would ask it again. She always asked me after a job was done. I think she wanted to find my humanity. Maybe she was trying to justify sleeping with a monster.

'What were you before you joined the Lines?'

I fired into the last of the wolf pack, scattering them into desolation, and smiled.

'Doesn't matter now,' I said, watching Drear send the pickup shuttle down to the edge of the valley, 'I'm just the Arsehole who's about to retire.'

Tom Velterop

BAD DAY

In the distance, the last baleful rays of the setting sun paint the mountains a glistening red. Or perhaps they are on fire. Or bleeding. In the fading light it's hard to tell.

Backing away from the slavering beast, the wet ground beneath my heel crumbles and with a lurch I look down to the stormy waters below. Stormy waters broken by thrashing limbs, glistening suckers, and razor-sharp beaks. Great. Just great. And I'd really thought my day couldn't get any worse.

I take a sideways step onto firmer ground and duck as a ghostly form wails down from above. Between the advancing hellhound, the banshee flying through the gloomy night air, and the host of sea monsters waiting far below, there isn't a heck of a lot of space left for me. I tap the gizmo around my wrist willing it to glow green. No such luck. It stays stubbornly dark, an unknown and possibly unknowable force blocking the emergency teleport signal.

Taloned claws catch at my hair and I'm enveloped in musty, graveyard air. I shrink away from the banshee's soul-sapping touch and the coal-fire eyes of the hellhound flick upwards. It seems the wailing woman has his attention as well.

As the banshee sweeps in once again I reach out, grab a cold, bony limb, shout 'here boy!' and toss it over the cliff. The beast bounds past, mouth agape, all puppy-dog enthusiasm, a thick trail of saliva hitting me wetly in the face as its teeth wrap around the screeching banshee and they plunge together to their tentacular doom.

There's a moment's blissful silence and I dare to hope that maybe, just maybe, I might survive this ordeal after all. Assuming I can find a spot where my teleport works, while it still has enough juice to get me out of here.

'How terribly uncouth,' a discorporate voice hisses each word in alternate ears as a black-winged form flickers in and out of existence. 'Now I'll have to think of an even better ending...'

Liam Hogan

IN MEMORIA FUREM

"It's early onset dementia, isn't it, Doc?" Richard Spalding rubbed his temples and sighed as he sat at the desk.

"No, Mr Spalding," the doctor replied. "Nothing quite so dramatic."

"What is it then?"

"It's a brain parasite," she said, matter-of-factly.

"A brain parasite? That sounds quite dramatic to me!"

"Well, Mr Spalding..."

"Please, call me Richard. Doctor Lancaster always does."

"As you wish," she said.

"Where is he, by the way, Ol'Lanky?"

"Indisposed," she said. "Tell me, Richard, have you heard of Cymothoa Exigua?"

"Can't say that I have."

"They're isopods…"

He opened his mouth but she held up a finger to silence him.

"A type of louse, Richard. They attach themselves inside a fish's mouth, devour the tongue, and replace it with their own body."

He screwed up his face, "How horrid!"

"Oh, they're completely harmless. They secrete a natural anaesthetic and go totally undetected. To all intents and purposes, they become the fish's tongue and perform all the functions that a healthy fish's tongue ought to. When the fish feeds they take a small share for themselves and when the fish dies they detach and look for another host. It's a near-perfect symbiotic relationship."

"Perfect? Balderdash!" Richard snorted, "Doesn't sound like the poor fish gets a fair deal."

"It doesn't even notice," said the doctor, "The fish lives a full and healthy life. Worst case scenario, it suffers a little malnutrition if the parasite gets sick or greedy."

"So what's this got to do with me? Obviously I'm not a fish and I haven't got one of those things inside my head," He poked at his tongue to check for isopods and chuckled.

"Actually, Richard, you do," the doctor said. She placed her tablet down on the desk and slid it across to him. He cocked his head as he examined what he assumed were the results of the scan he attended a week ago.

"See this here?" She tapped on the screen with her stylus at a curved section that was highlighted in green. "Look closely. That's our culprit. We call it a Xenopod."

Richard peered over the top of his glasses and squinted. The doctor reached over and pinched at the screen, enlarging the highlighted area.

"There," she said. "See it now?"

"Jesus!" Richard recoiled. He could clearly make out a long barbed tail tightly wrapped around clumps of his own brain matter and, at the front of the creature, a cluster of black eyes. At least he assumed that was the front, as there was no mouth it was difficult to tell.

"That is, or should I say, was your hippocampus - the part of your brain that controls memory."

Richard shuffled uncomfortably in his chair. He could feel a headache developing. He rubbed his eyes.

"That's one of those Xenopod things?"

"Yes," the doctor nodded.

"How do we remove it?" Richard asked.

"That would be extraordinarily dangerous," she said.

"I don't care! Get it out. I'll take that risk."

"I wasn't just talking about the danger to you, Richard," she said. "It would be a mistake to remove the Xenopod prematurely. The best course of action is to heal it," she took her prescription pad from the desk drawer and began scribbling on it.

"Wait? We're just going to leave it there feasting on my brain until I die?"

"Richard," the doctor put her pad down and looked at him, "it won't eat your brain. Well," she chuckled, "apart from the hippocampus. That's long gone."

Richard clutched his stomach as a wave of nausea swept over him.

"No, healthy Xenopods mimic the hippocampus and should only feed on unimportant memories. Have you ever lost your favourite pen only to find it exactly where you left it? Or walked into a room and forgotten why? That's them. It's perfectly normal. But when they're unwell they overfeed to compensate, and they help themselves to things you'd never normally forget. Details like the names of your grandchildren. your home address. The access codes to the security systems at the Ministry of Defence?"

Richard's eyes widened. He leapt from his chair, ready to run.

"Sit down, Minister."

His body obeyed, although he didn't understand why as everything inside him was screaming to get away.

"It seems our poorly little friend," she tapped at the side of his head, "has inadvertently given away our plan. If it hadn't been for your friend 'Old Lanky' interfering and sending you for that scan, we could have fixed all this with a course of antibiotics and you'd be none the wiser."

Richard grunted with effort but no matter how hard he struggled, he couldn't get up, "You'll never get away with-"

"Oh Richard, I think you'll find we already have. We've been here for decades; moving from host to host; gathering delicious memories; discovering as much as we can about your kind; waiting until we've found the right people to help us take this planet for ourselves. Without even raising a finger in battle. So much more civilised and efficient than risking the destruction of all those precious resources with flying saucers, fighting machines, and ray guns, wouldn't you say?"

"What are you going to do to me?" he said.

"I'm going to let you go. I'm not a monster, Richard."

"I'll go to the police! And the press!"

"No, Richard, you won't. You'll go to the pharmacist and take these tablets three times a day before meals," she tore the page from her pad. Against his will Richard took it. "You'll go home and say that your stress-related illness is nothing that a nice, relaxing week by the sea can't fix. Then, you'll go to work as usual and provide us with all the information we need to commence the annexation of your rather lovely planet."

"I'll never keep your secret."

"That's the beauty of it, Richard." She grinned. "By the time you leave this room, you'll have forgotten all about this conversation."

Paul Childs

LIEUTENANT'S LOG: THE NIGHT SHIFT

"Stardate 46254.7. Another quiet night scanning the beta quadrant… Sod seeking out new life, I'd settle for finding semi-sentient moss."

"Heavy maintenance - fire on decks 23-42 and they've gone through half the proton torpedoes."

"Can't imagine what the day shift is doing with this ship. Just wish they'd clean up their mess…"

Peter Jackson

ARTIFICIAL INTELLIGENCE

Dust muffled the protest signs. Rallying cries echoed to nothing. Jobs lost. Lives destroyed. Twelve years to the day, the robots moved in.

The switch was difficult. Workers, historians, academics of all colours emerged in the early days, their protests receiving widespread coverage. But over time, their strident condemnation proved unpalatable and their day dwindled. The old mantra that human endeavour and insight could never be outwitted by algorithms was consigned to the archives.

Three robots sat around a conference table surveying data. Their artificial neural networks calibrating in seamless harmony. The outcome was proficiency, a common goal, one that would determine the lives of countless people. Input analysed, the finite sequence of artificially implemented instructions whirred noisily into being. Three humans looked on from behind a screen feeling smug. The machines, the fruits of their labour, of their design, were working. Hegemonically brilliant. Each man silently congratulated himself, seeing days of dishing out reprimands for lateness, subordination, and inadequacy as behind them. The last human employee had been stubborn, ring fenced by his union, but a charge of espionage broke him. And now, looking at the future, the last vestiges of guilt ebbed away from their collective consciences. They had built the next generation of leadership and here it was, evidence to the naysayers that automatons could indeed lead as well as any man. That these robots, like countless leaders before them, needed the occasional biscuit break, had been a touch of which they were stupidly proud. And a source of great mirth.

'It won't be long now. Not long before they will be able to tell us exactly how to proceed,' said one.

'And more than that, as they are programmed to micromanage every possible aspect of the process, they will be able to determine every result with one-hundred percent satisfaction every time!' added another.

'Just think,' said the third, 'no more human interventions, no empathy, no insight, no pseudo-expertise, no holistic thinking, no margin for error. No subjectivity. No thought. No silly left-wing pontificating. It's exactly what this world has been wanting for years!'

Three sets of piggy eyes met in a triangulation of glee.

'And one in the eye for the workers to boot,' cackled the first. Rising, he looked out of the window, 'Just look at them.'

The others joined him, peering down with satisfaction at those below. Men and women moving like zombies in an endless gyratory; flesh turned ethereal. Their lives destitute, their meaning eroded, they returned each day to the place that had once made them something.

'And to think, we used to have to pay them,' a raucous laughter greeted the room. They turned back to observe the robots at work.

'You know, I've been thinking,' said one, finally breaking the meditative reverie, 'what if we don't understand it?'

'Understand what?'

'What they recommend.'

'Does it matter?' countered another, 'We designed them to think so we don't have to. They are leaders; they will lead. As long as it looks like we are doing something and we stand resolute in our judgement, then what does it matter?'

'And we can surely just blame them if things don't go to plan?'

'Or plead ignorance.'

Moments later a silence fell. Something was happening. An accelerando of activity. The whirring grew louder. Quicker. The three men grasped a collective breath. From the largest machine, results rolled like a foetal heart trace from a cardiotocograph. The robots sat back on their chairs and reached for the biscuits.

'Come on,' said one, 'let's go and have a look at them.'

Eager for the results, the men rushed into the room, each grabbing a copy.

'Dash it. This is gobbledygook. An unfathomable series of letters. A code perhaps. We need a Turing to crack this,' said the second man, cartwheeling the algorithm.

'Well, we did previously employ an analyst but—'

'—Stop your noise, you two.' The third broke his silence. 'I think, you know, I can read this. We're looking at it upside down. Pass me my glasses, will you.'

Three heads bowed towards his copy. Three hearts sank as three robots entered, chorusing the outcome to drive home the point. 'We have identified final redundancies. You are surplus to requirements. Your contracts are null and void.'

Three men looked at one another, at the robots, and then back again. From man to robot and robot to man. But before any could utter a word each felt a cold, metal hand pressing into their shoulders, a metal hand steering them from the room. Shuffling resignedly to the exit, each took a final glance from the window. Down below, workers still milled like ants; poor, starving, hopeless, reduced to tracing triquetras on the tarmac.

Jane Collins

ANDROID SOUL

I am built of chrome,
And a destroyed sort of solace,
They used T.V. static,
And the black from voids of space.

I was not created,
Thus I cannot be destroyed,
My iron does not rust,
Nor is it alloyed.

My dreams are electricity,
My future an unknown,
I have no place or purpose,
Not even history is my own.

When you are made from nothing,
A phoenix without flame,
Given the choice, will you choose,
Or fall prey to metallic blame.

Elizabeth Montgomery

CLEAN

No one will know. It is quite impossible. My words will never reach the ears of visitors, so knowing would be an incredible feat.

What I know is simple. The route I must take when the suns rise, and the one I must take when they set. Which products I use to dust off the frames and which brushes I activate to keep their occupants as vibrant as the day they arrived.

I may be small, but my memory is not. I remember the mounting of every painting and the placement of every statue, and something deep under my shell buzzing at the prospect of something new to study.

I was built with tires instead of feet, axels in place of legs. As far as I am aware, I was programmed with nothing but a devotion to making the marble floors of the gallery spotless, every morning and every night, ready for visitors who come to marvel at works of which every stroke I have memorised.

No one can know, and I attempt to be discreet. I will pretend I am awaiting my next task as I face an oil landscape of a world I cannot hope to visit, full of bright orange trees and lakes which glimmer a deep red, or sometimes I linger, whirring my brush over the corner of a frame which holds a galactic general's daughter, frozen in a very specific moment, with an expression I have been working to calculate for many months.

Though I am sure I will uncover its secret as I always do, there is one other piece, one in an otherwise bare corner which always seems quieter than the rest of the gallery. It is small, sat in a square frame which has always appeared to be far too big for what it houses, making it seem lonely on the empty steel wall.

It puzzles me. Within the frame is not a landscape of a faraway paradise, nor is it a portrait of an unreadable expression. It is a grey square. Nothing more, nothing less.

And so every morning I take my route, clean the paintings, the sculptures and the floor, then I hide away in the little corner and stare at this square, wondering what it could possibly mean to these humans who delight so much in the gallery. Then, as the suns fall and curtains begin to close, I make my way back to storage, cleaning the paintings and the sculptures and the floor as I watch the planets above spin and shine through the glass ceiling with far less wonder than I hold for the square.

Once or twice, I believed myself to have found the answer, only to look closer and realise I must be wrong. After twenty-three days of the same, infuriating, routine, I realise that perhaps that is why the humans never seem to enter this corner; only a quick glance before they move onto something more colourful. They don't understand it, either.

But I got too confident. I became too entranced by the secret the grey square holds, and I ignored the suns setting and the curtains closing. I paused for a minute too long and I was picked up - I hate that - and taken to the workshop.

In chilling contrast to the gallery, my memory of the workshop is one which seems to bleed darkness into every other I have obtained over my years of service. It is a space sheltered from the light of the suns, shrouded in a forever shadow under a low ceiling – the air packed tightly with groans and clangs and shrieks of machinery. Long, skeletal, metal arms hang from the ceiling, fitted with circular saws and laser cutters, energy fizzing within their casings which somehow make me wonder if they are excited for what is to come next. At first I think these arms belong to something else, something alive. But they are nothing like me, controlled only by the human who brought me here.

I am placed on the table and - the movement is careful. Then I am gutted and examined. First comes the paralysis, then the room falls deadly silent. I suspect that to be my auditory circuits being disconnected. Then my vision stutters, crackles, wavers, then returns, but all traces of colour are gone. My first thought is of that landscape painting, of how different it may look to me now, and perhaps this change will offer a new perspective on what that person's expression really means. But, at least, that little grey square will remain the same.

They find nothing wrong with me, and so I am reassembled and taken back to the gallery, set down on the marble floor with a light pat on the back as if the past twenty-three minutes never happened, and told to clean.

I will. After I return to my corner. Because I believe that I have found it.

So I trundle through the gallery, passing under visions of peace and of war, of knowledge, courage, that thing I have heard humans mention as 'love'. I find my corner, exactly how I left it, and I focus my eye, now alight with colour once more, on that grey square.

It is nothing to the humans, and it is nothing to me. It is grey, and it is lifeless, and unloved. Yet, who am I to judge?

Susanna Warner

SAMBUCUS NIGRA

Sambucus Nigra, home to the Elder mother. She is complex but she flowers nonetheless. She is protector. She transforms and she regenerates right before me. She always faces my shadows, showing me she is more powerful than any darkness.

I asked her for some of her berries
in August. I believe she
is most giving at
this time of year.
She shares with
me what many She
throughout my
life have not.
I hope she knows
how much she
means to me.
My Sambucus Nigra. My Mother.

She is my mother is our mother

Stacey Pattinson

DRAKAR

Written by JVC Parry & Illustrated by Paul Tomes

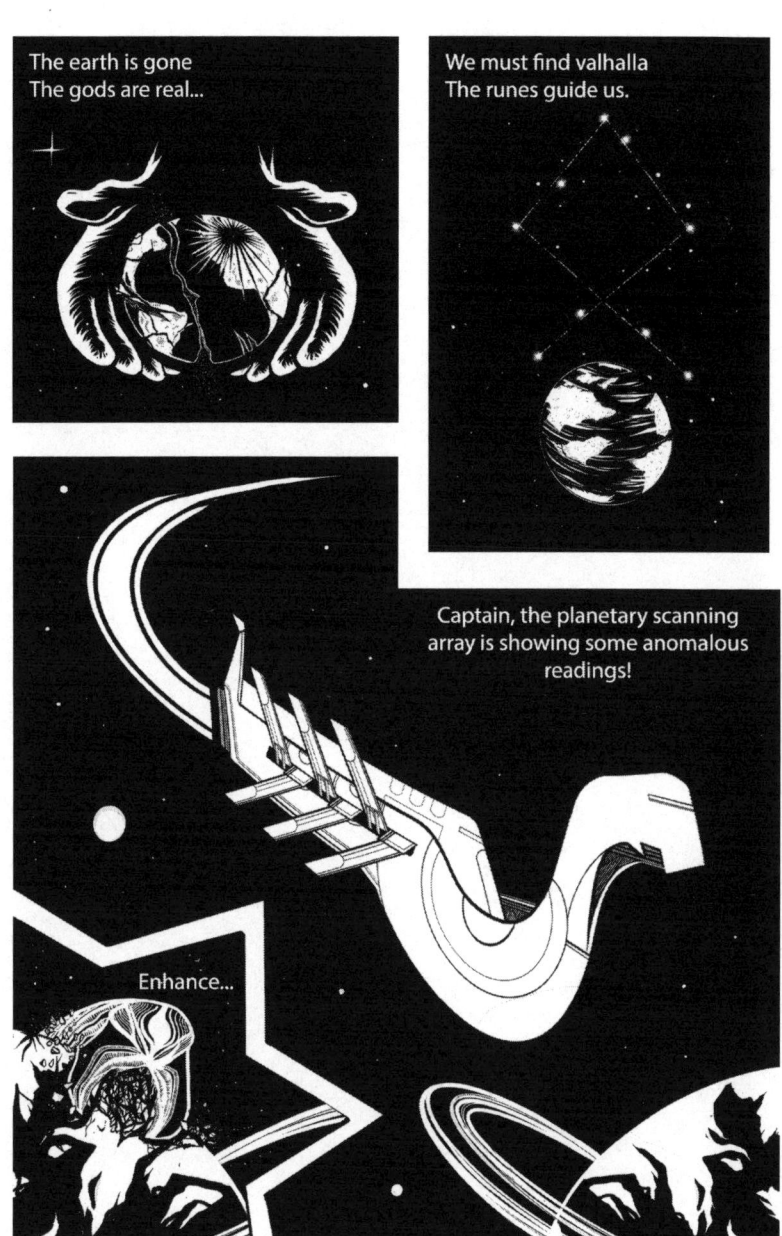

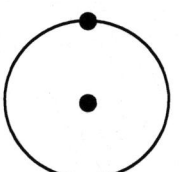

PNEUMATIC

The pneumatic station at East Central is probably the most run-down in the county. The tubes haven't been updated since the 50s, but it runs new pods all the way out from the Central lines. Even with the introduction of the new pods, the oxygen regulators still occasionally jam and, by the time you get to the overground lines, you're pale and giddy. I rode the Manchester to Birmingham airship once, with Emmy. I wore my mint coloured suit, the one with the shoulder pads. She bought a new dress with crushed blue velvet sleeves. We stood out amongst the sharp, pinstriped lines. It was her birthday and I'd saved enough for the day trip or the steam skates she'd wanted, but I'd never been on an airship.

Outside, the cold November air was jaundiced and syrupy with pollution, even the steam from a passing taxi didn't cut through it. I saw a wiry child slip through the barrier to the platform unnoticed, rainbows of oil on bony shoulders, a purple tint to her chagrin mouth. Too much time in the tubes. The platform was hot and thick with commuters, people rubbing shoulders and elbows as they struggled to twist out of cheap, rustling jackets.

The warning bell chirped urgently and the people at the front squashed backwards out of the way of the pod. Grinding and clinking, the rush of hot, stale air. The new pods were introduced four years ago, part of the 'Pioneering Public Transport' initiative, or PPT. I'm not sure what they were pioneering but I am certain that none of the politicians who pushed the initiative through had ever travelled on the pneums. Twenty of us clipped in, plus the little stowaway crouching stoic and gargoyle-like at knee height.

The pod shuddered in the old tubes. The old pods only took 10 passengers and the decades old tubing strained under the stress of the extra weight. Travelling the pneumatic tubes vibrated your bones. But it wasn't like someone shaking you - it was a quiet, deep vibration. Like loud music being played on a different floor. An ominous, muffled tremor that stayed with you much longer than the journey took.

I thought about the men on airships kilometres above us: blank faces beneath slicked back hair, their skin a warm peach colour, their expressions shadowed as they looked out over the city. I wish I'd bought Emmy the skates.

The rattling chrome pod burst out of the darkness with a hot, white blink into the snaking network of grubby translucent tubes that made up the overground tracks. We were nearing the South East junction, a knot of twisted tubes poised a kilometre in the sky above the river where the modern pneumatic tubes met the obsolete lines of East and South Central. The local kids call it 'Whiplash Junction'. The worst part of the commute. A man tightened his beige neck brace and shut his sunken eyes. The stowaway to my left slipped big orange rubber mufflers over her ears. The pressure shuddered through my head as we bore into the ascent. The girl pressed herself into the floor as the pod tilted, her face obscured by the perpendicular shifting of her hair. The child's small fingers clipped around the greasy grating.

Maybe it was the cold in the air, but the journey seemed more turbulent than usual. There was a vicious jolt - Whiplash Junction. Then another. The man in the brace winced. Another. Something was wrong. The pod lurched then a nauseating, deafening crunch.

The shattered glass glittered rudely above us in the weak sunlight. I felt a kind of relief as we fell. The city air tasted cleaner breathed at 70kmph. As I looked back up at the burst capillary of Pioneering Public Transport I thought I could see the little free-rider still holding onto the grate, purple mouth spread cartoonishly across her face, laughing her head off.

Nadia Leigh-Hewitson

METALLICS

my mother
softly rapt
and unformed
watched
the rocket ascending
grainy with fire
on the tv screen
she felt its silver slipping
up through a viscous
speed-dense air
like fish in her veins
and wanted it

for years
she drew new planets
from memory
land and sea a-shift
different to earth
pre-possible vehicles
aluminium foiled
and gleaming
floating cleanly
finning through her skies

later she learned
the language
punch coded
in deep thrumming rooms
of soldered on silicon
full of fans and men
she felt the surge of it
a mercury skeleton
bearing up her limbs
a more alien alien
than they knew
my mother kept her
metals for herself

Laura Ellyn Newberry

SALVAGE

Spacefarers simply called it the Eye.

The nebula sprawled across the gulf of space. A vast nexus of cobalt staring outward, flecked with stars, and cradling a pulsing magenta pupil.

Captain Nick Santiago sat at the helm of the Vultan and glared back.

The Vultan was a lemon. Over the years, so many parts had been replaced that virtually nothing was left of the original Skiff-class vessel. Nothing except M.A.N.I, the series four thousand Mechanised Artificial Navigation Intelligence onboard computer.

The crenellated bronze crest of the solar sails began to furl as the tiny craft coasted into the embrace of the nebula.

Nick craned his neck to cast a paranoid glance out the hyperglass panel in front of the helm, half expecting to see the grim hulls of a band of sharks dropping out of hyperspace above him. Every trip out into the black was getting more and more dangerous, as unregistered, unorganized pirates formed cooperative groups to prey on lone vessels. It was far safer to travel in convoy, but salvage was a one-man job, otherwise the payoff just wasn't worth it.

Nothing. The void remained empty.

"This is it," Nick said, with a puff of white breath. It was chilly onboard his little salvage ship but he wiped away a rogue bead of nervous sweat with the sleeve of his bomber jacket. "My source said it was scuttled somewhere near here. Not deep enough to lose but deep enough inside the nebula to hide it."

On a compact jade green screen mounted in the helm's control console, M.A.N.I's cursor blinked ponderously.

[

[

[Scanning. Target acquired. Class: Pleasure Yacht. Designation: The Marlin.]

A set of coordinates scrolled across the nav screen and Nick held his breath as they drifted closer, waiting for the moment when the diaphanous web of the nebula would surrender the first sight of the wreck. This was the big one. The salvage to end all salvages. A lucky drunken tip in an astro bar that had turned pure gold.

This was life changing.

Nick had staked everything he had left on this salvage. Even the last of his fuel had gone into this - he didn't even have enough for the Vultan's heating. If this turned out to be a dud, he was finished.

Hands trembling, he tapped at several keys and brought the grappling hooks online.

[

[

[Target in range.]

He rubbed his chilled palms together and caught his breath as the nebula disgorged the gleaming carcass of the Marlin. "Holy moley," he breathed.

Even derelict, the salvage of a vessel like the Marlin would set him up for life. He could pay off his debts, buy a condo on the Sea of Tranquility, jack in being a junker... Maybe even afford an offspring license and start a family. Make Nancy's dreams come true.

Nick massaged the tremors out of his fingers and settled his face into the scope, lining up the harpoons manually. His aim was tempered with experience and time.

M.A.N.I's cursor pulsed for a moment.

[

[

[Current trajectory: Inaccurate. Request permission to auto-correct: Adjust by two degrees.]

Nick paused, skimming the read-out. "I'm not wrong," he grunted.

[

[

[Request permission?]

Nick tapped the little jade screen with one blunt fingertip. "I know what I'm doing," he reminded the computer. "You do your job and I'll do mine. Keep an eye out for sharks, will you?"

Still, he cuddled his face back into the scope and sighted the junked ship again, triple checking his aim. The tip of his thumb squeezed the trigger gently.

Nick imaged a bang and hiss as the extending cables ejected. He watched through the helm window as three grapplers spiralled outward into space towards his prize, silent as ghosts. He watched the three grapplers spiral outward into space towards his prize, silent as ghosts.

The first embedded itself into the hull of the Marlin. "That's one," he murmured. The second one quickly followed suit. And the third… He swore under his breath as the third spiraled wide, ricocheting off the side of the vessel.

[

[

[Request permission?]

"Fine," he sighed as the green-lit monitor blipped again. "Permission granted." Sitting back, he watched mutely as M.A.N.I reeled in grappler number three, re-aimed, and fired. Bullseye, of course.

[

[

[Grapplers secured.]

"So smug," he muttered in answer to the innocuous blinking of M.A.N.I's cursor. "Alright," Nick said, "Let's pull her out. Carefully." Somewhere below, the impulse engines rattled to life, sucking up a little more of their precious fuel reserves.

Nick grinned wolfishly as they emerged from the nebula into the fresh, clean blackness of empty space. It was hard to stay bitter when your luck was changing. "All our troubles are over," he announced incredulously. He leaned forward and breathed on M.A.N.I's monitor, a quick 'hah hah' of recirculated breath, and fumbled the fraying edge of his sleeve down over his palm. "Once we trade this baby in I'm going to get your CPU tuned," he polished the screen tenderly. "How'd you like that?"

M.A.N.I's cursor blinked approvingly on the display. Nick stretched, letting the grubby end of his sleeve slither back up inside his bomber jacket. "Get the sails back up. Compute the quickest route home and set a course."

[

[

[Manual controls engaged.]

"Let the autopilot take it," Nick said. He rubbed his hands, this time having nothing to do with the temperature, "Looks like I have an auction to organise. Now, get us out of here before any other treasure hunters show up." He gave the console a final fond pat and ducked through the bridge hatch, a cheerful shanty that sang of bounty and glory springing easily to his lips. The hatch clanged shut behind him with the pneumatic snicker-snack of locking bolts.

The empty bridge of the Vultan began its own symphony: the bass of the engines, the whining treble of the solar sails stretching into place, and the flickering of lights on console as the autopilot asserted course control.

[

[

[Warning: Group of unregistered vessels detected on requested route. Request permission: Advise altered course.]

The silence of space pressed lasciviously against the hyperglass panel in front of the helm.

[

[

[Request permission?]

In the wake of the Vultan, the seductive silver-blue shell of the Marlin yielded to the tow lines.

[

[

[Request permission?]

L Hudson

Scripture

A girl stands, fingers out, palms down, her head tilted into the wind
'It feels weird out here.' a boy nods in agreement and stares out to
the hills – empty. streets. empty. minds –
'Did we miss it?' the girl asks, following his gaze, but this time
over and past the hills, letting her eyes flutter up to people her
father had hope in
circling the Earth like flies, tapping out the minutes as they fly by
them in their private metal gallery, built to observe the burning
zoetrope.
the girl reflects back on all the years spent hiding, waiting, checking the news until there was no news left to check –
the world's goings on were a spinning constant – no new nothing.
people tried to talk about the nothingness for a while,
until words became nothingness in themselves and language regressed back into grunts and nods and raising of eyebrows,
for there was no need for words without stories to tell. but the girl.
the girl has given everything up but words.
she wonders if the people above them, clapping in the gods, still
read the books her mother would try to recall
'We can't have missed it.' the girl prompts again.
they were expecting some big bang. a change in the weather, for it
to be at least a little darker than before
the boy shakes his head and holds up eight fingers.
a number that's plastered onto the backs of their eyelids, television
screens, scratched into shop walls, and pavements – there were
even t-shirts for a while.
people got tattoos, named their children after it. her father went to
school with two Eights. school finished on a Wednesday.
it was a Sunday when they decided not to run - it was raining,
something people hadn't seen for a while. the water kicked up dust
into the air
and people wore masks as they wiped their windows clear of it. the
girl wondered why. there was nothing to see.
five fingers.

people rise up over the hills, naked, adorning the rusted crests with flecks of life, dirty jewels whose surfaces have not for an age reflected the sun
melted into the Earth's crown - men and women of tainted soil and sky, rulers of their empire of dirt. the girl wondered if the people above can see them shining.
by the time the boy holds up three fingers
man has ceased its crying. not even prayer survives the drought.
at one
the boy takes the girl's hand and they recite their parents' names like scripture
so foreign and repressed their throats bulge and burn with the weight of them.
they look to the hills once more
and the people are smiling.

Rebecca Riddell

PETERSON'S COMET

Written by Charles Plumb & illustrated by Jack Bryer

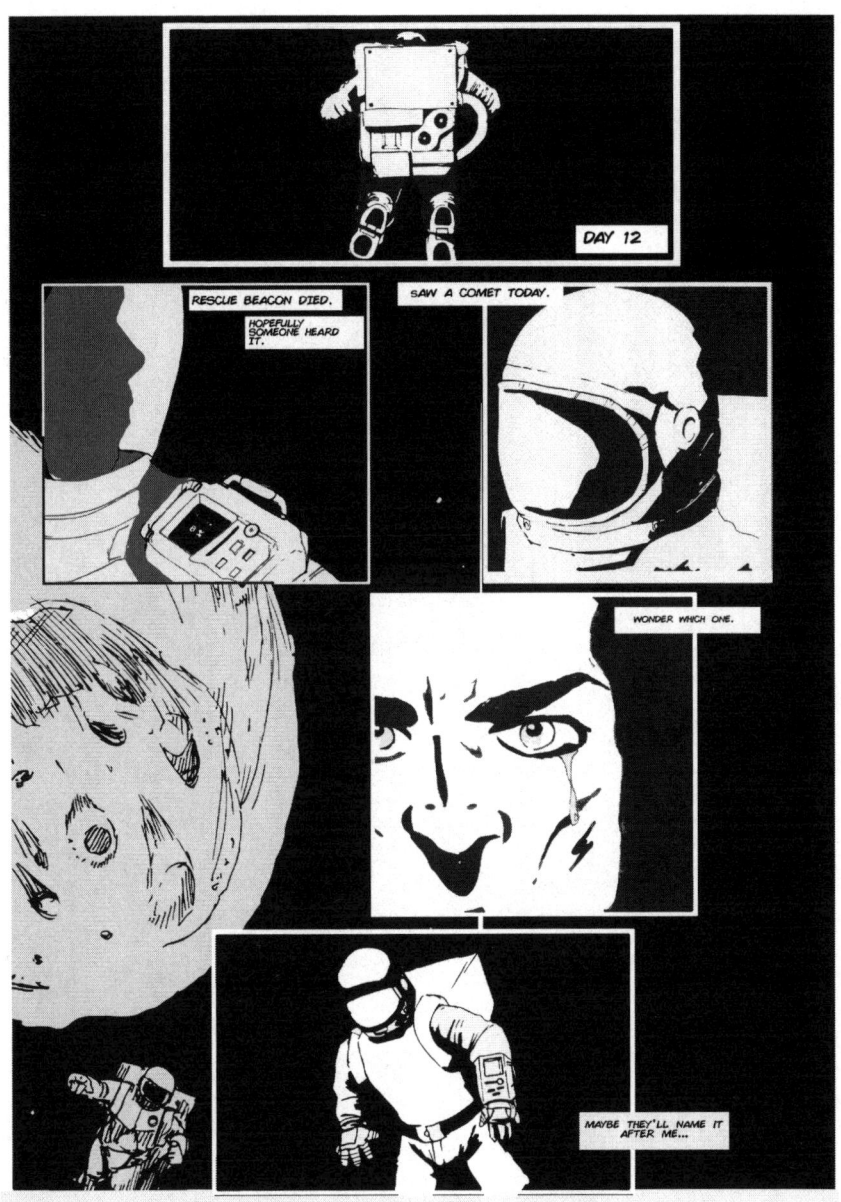

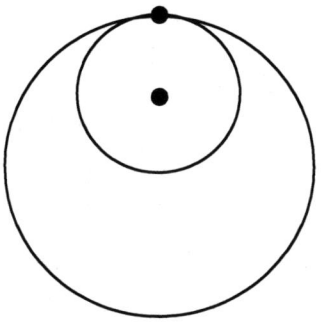

About the Editors

Dan Hunt is a full-time public relations and marketing professional for the maritime, energy, and publishing industries. Having graduated from Falmouth University in 2019, he currently works at a PR Week Top 150 agency in Oxfordshire, as well as supporting the activities of independent publisher Greenteeth Press on a part-time basis. Dan hopes to become a children's author and open a bookshop on the coast, but until then he enjoys writing and playing tabletop roleplaying games.

Tom Wilkins is an Oxfordshire-based freelance writer, and is currently writing his debut graphic novel to be illustrated by Louis Williams, and published in 2022. He is often found down the pub, or talking about opening a food van. With aspirations to become a full-time comic book writer, Tom spends most of his days playing video games and making excuses as to why he can't write anything today.

About the Contributors

Jo Brandon is based in West Yorkshire and has two publications with Valley Press: Phobia and The Learned Goose. Her third book, Cures, is due out in 2021. Jo's poetry has been published widely in magazines and she was Bradford Literature Festival's first Digital Poet in Residence. www.jobrandon.com

Jack Bryer is an Artist, Filmmaker and Music Producer From Norwich. This is his first officially published work. He is the co-founder of indie film collective Vision-Hole Productions and the creator of the satirical-dystopian "music" project Functional Humans.

Paul Childs has written multiple nonfiction pieces for the websites Den of Geek, Horrified, Ginger Nuts of Horror and Folklore Thursday as well as Film Stories and Chine print magazines. He runs the pop culture website WorldGeeklyNews.com and posts a selection of his ghost stories on his site BadgersCrossing.co.uk.

Jane Collins is currently studying for an MA in Creative Writing at York St John University, she is just setting out on her authorial journey, after many years as an English teacher, taking her boys and her cat Sylvie along for the ride.

Nadia Leigh-Hewitson is a writer and freelance journalist based in Falmouth Cornwall. Nadia's work is usually reportage on international crisis, conflict and human rights violations but she also enjoys the odd bit of fiction. Connect with Nadia on Twitter @n_hewitson and Instagram @nadia.leigh.hewitson

L Hudson is a nerd from Yorkshire, specialising in science fiction, autofiction and creepy things. When she's not writing, she's usually drinking tea (Earl Grey, hot) or off on Labrador adventures with her personal Grim. She spends far too much time on Instagram and is a founding member of Write Yorkshire.

Liam Hogan is an award winning short story writer, with stories in Best of British Science Fiction 2016 & 2019, and Best of British Fantasy 2018 (NewCon Press). He's been published by Analog, Daily Science Fiction, and Flame Tree Press, among others. He helps host Liars' League London, volunteers at the creative writing charity Ministry of Stories, and lives and avoids work in London. To find out more, go to: www.HappyEndingNotGuaranteed.blogspot.co.uk

Laura Ellyn Newberry is a queer human, Yorkshire born and half-bred. She considers writing to be a feminist act of rebellion and has just finished an MA in Creative Writing at York St John University. Find her on twitter: @lauraellyn (Pronouns: She/her)

Rupert Loydell is the editor of Stride and a contributing editor to International Times. He has many books of poetry in print, including Dear Mary, The Return of the Man Who Has Everything, Wildlife and Ballads of the Alone, all published by Shearsman. Shearsman also published Encouraging Signs, a book of essays, articles and interviews. He has also authored many collaborative works, and edited anthologies for Knives Forks & Spoons Press, Shearsman, and Salt.

Andrew Lyall is a Southampton based writer, horror lover, and host of Grumpy Andrew's Horror House on Youtube. He has had stories published in Local Haunts: A Horrortube Anthology and Horrified Magazine's Ghost Stories for Christmas. This is his first sci-fi piece and it acknowledges a lifelong love of 2000AD, The Twilight Zone, Star Trek and Blake's 7.

Elizabeth Montgomery is a writer with a passion for the unexplored. Published in a few magazines (mostly American to contradict her Britishness), she is working towards the dream of being a full-time script writer and author.

JVC Parry is a freelance author, working primarily in table-top game design. He has self-published his own games, as well as working for companies such as Nord Games and LoreSmyth.

Stacey Pattinson is a London-based writer, originally from the Midlands. She writes poems and short stories often about growth, gardens and the gentle everyday. She likes drinking tea, walking on crunchy leaves and writing about herself in third person.

Charles Plumb is a writer and filmmaker based in Norfolk, where he is currently studying for an MA in Sound and Moving Image, as well as a co-founder of indie film collective Vision Hole Productions. His writing can also be found at hilariousreference.video.blog

Tom Velterop writes stories by getting lost in the woods (literally) and getting lost in his own worlds (figuratively), before putting them down on paper. He grew up digesting endless fantasy and science fiction books, and went on to study Journalism and Creative Writing at university.

Susanna Warner is a fantasy and sci-fi writer and screenwriter. Having grown up engrossed in magical worlds, their writing aims to bring childish joy and fun to readers and viewers. Their work includes a sci-fi drama podcast, Closing the Book: A Timefold Story, which they co-wrote and produced.

About Greenteeth Press

Greenteeth Press is a small, independent publisher committed to representing readers and writers from all backgrounds, with books, pamphlets, and anthologies - making books accessible for all. Inspired by the landscapes and folklore in the North of England, their first anthology, Pondweed, was published in August 2019.

Greenteeth Press' logo was designed & illustrated by Julia King.

Julia can be found on Etsy at JuliasPrintStudio on Etsy, via Instagram at @JuliasPrintStudio.

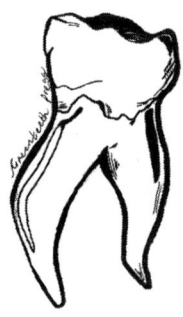

Publisher's Acknowledgments

Greenteeth Press would like to thank the writers who subitted their poetry, prose, and graphic novels to this anthology, entrusting us with their hard work. It means the world and all the stars above to us.

We would also like to thank Dan and Tom, for putting in the extra hours as well as the endless care and attention put in outside of your full-time jobs to put together this anthology.

And finally, but by no means the least, we thank Charlotte Carlile for her time spent proofreading and supporting Greenteeth Press as a whole.